Walking in grandma's garden

by Bobbie Roman
illustrated by Lorelei Kirsch

edited by Joyce Kirsch
photographs by Lorelei Kirsch and Bobbie Roman

When I became 60
I did not run in a marathon
Or climb a mountain.
I gardened.
And wrote a book about it
For our grandchildren.

Many thanks to my encouraging, supportive family and friends; and a special thank you to Fran, Pat, Lorelei and Joyce.

—B.R.

Thank you flowers, green leaves and summer bugs. You have taught me patience.

—L.K.

First Edition, Second Printing
All rights reserved.
Copyright © 1998 Stargazer Publishing

ISBN Number: 0-9668846-0-4

Library of Congress Catalog Card Number: 98-96901

Summary: Following the stepping stones through grandma's garden, children are introduced to flowers and ecology in a fun, familiar format.

Published by:
Stargazer Publishing
455 Eastwood Drive
Stevens Point, WI 54481

Printed in the United States of America by:
Palmer Publications, Inc.
318 N. Main Street
Amherst, WI 54406

Some children call their grandmother
Grandma. Others call her Nanna,
or Nonna, or Busha, or Oma.
What do you call *your* grandmother?

Whatever names they are called, family and
flowers are favorites of mine. So are books.
Let's you and I walk the path through this
book to see what's happening in
Grandma's garden.

These yellow
Iris (EYE ris)
smell lemony.

Iris leaves are like
swords—sharp on
the edges.

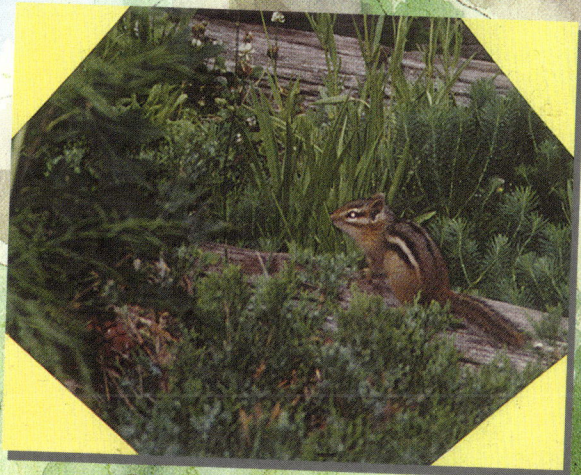

Peonies (PEE oh nees),
pink and plush as cotton candy.

Sometimes they have a sweet
sticky something on
their stems. . .ants love it!

Chipmunks chase around the Astilbe (ah STILL bee) and Petunias (pet UNE ee yuhs).

Purple Coneflower can
be used as medicine, to
soothe a cold. . .or ease
a tummy ache.

Bleeding Hearts are
shaped like hearts, but
they don't bleed.

Yarrow (YAH row)

nestles near

Wooly Lamb's Ears.

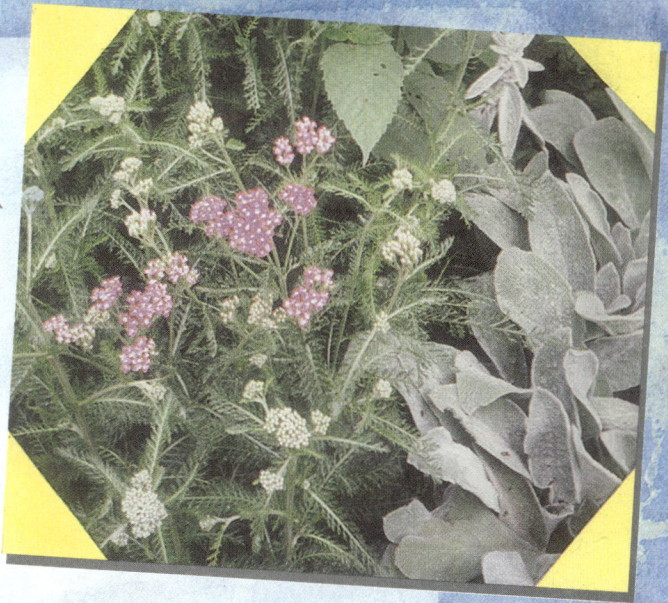

Some other flowers

with animal names are:

Goat's Beard, Turtlehead, and Pig Squeak.

The seed pod of
the Poppy
is filled with
tiny seeds.

Turn it over, shake it. . .
seeds sprinkle out
like pepper.

14

Bunnies like to eat Lavatera (lava TEA ruh)—

I like to look at it.

Queen Anne's Lace
looks like snowflakes,
or umbrellas for dolls.

Creeping Phlox
bloom in spring,
covering their stems
with a blanket
of flowers.

19

Some Hostas are small and some are HUGE.

Plant plenty, because the deer like to nibble them.

The Daylily tastes sweet.
It is crunchy and juicy to chew.

Other flowers you can eat are
Pansies, Lilac, and Tulip.
Always check with an adult
before eating any flower.

Can you find the bee
on the Daisy?

Daisy is also a girl's name.
Some other flowers with girl's
names are Marguerite, Jasmine,
Lily, and Rose.

24

Do you think there are flowers with boy's names?

(see glossary at back of book)

The garden is a busy place—

deer nibble, bees hover, bugs crawl,

butterflies flutter, birds flit,

chipmunks chase, and flowers grow.

Watch for them next time you visit your

grandma's garden.

More about grandma's garden. . .

IRIS (EYE ris). Our garden began with some simple, ordinary yellow iris. Then I added purple, a gift from a dear friend. This year, elegant bearded iris of many colors from another gardening friend gave us a stunning spring sight. Along the way, I finally smelled the yellow iris and was embarrassed to realize I had not known their lemony scent before. A new sense of appreciation for that "simple, ordinary" yellow iris!

PEONY *paeonia* (pee Oh nee a). Peonies are hardy, easy to grow, require little care, and last for years. They are dependable, relatively disease-free, have attractive foliage and extremely showy blooms. In other words, as close to the perfect perennial as there is. The only care my peonies have required is staking of the flower heads. They are top-heavy, especially when wet. Those that I don't stake, I cut—for spectacular bouquets.

HOSTA (HASS tuh) is another plant whose family has multiplied and been improved amazingly in recent years. I like the dramatic effect of hosta leaves in the shade garden and in bouquets.

PETUNIA (pet UNE ee yuh). A commonly seen annual, petunia is not so "common" anymore with its many new bushy and trailing varieties.

PURPLE CONEFLOWER *echinacea* (eck in AY see uh). Native Americans have long valued this plant for its medicinal, remedial qualities. Today we often hear herbalists proclaiming the healing properties of its roots. A friend brought me Echinacea tea when I was suffering from a bad cold. I felt better quickly, but attribute that as much to the thoughtfulness of a friend as to the medicinal power of the flower.

WARNING:

- Many plants have toxic properties and some are poisonous. Identify plants carefully. If you are uncertain, do not use as food or medicine.
- Remember, medicines taken in small quantities may be harmful in larger amounts.
- Consult a trusted, qualified health professional before treating yourself medically.

DAYLILY *hemorocallis* (hem er oh CAL iss). A popular plant that has been developed to include almost any color and many shapes. It has been used for centuries as ornament, food, and medicine. Our grandchildren love to offer daylily petals to unsuspecting visitors, insisting, "try it, really, it tastes good!"

LAMB'S EARS *stachys* (STACK iss). A plant that my grandchildren love to touch. I like stachys for filling in blank areas and as an edging plant. If the plant spreads too far too fast, just dig it up. And if you don't care for the flower, just cut it off. This year I transplanted some of the overgrowth to the edge of our woodland path. The shade is quite deep, but so far, the lamb's ears are surviving even there.

YARROW *achillea* (uh KILL ee uh). Another perennial with several varieties. Be careful, yarrow tends to take over in the garden.

LAVATERA (lav a TEA ruh). An annual resembling the perennial mallow family. The pink lavatera pictured had throats that glistened with a silvery hue. It was covered with blooms and would have lasted for weeks if the bunnies weren't so fond of them! If the bunnies like your lavatera also, don't give up. Consider it deadheaded and wait for the new blooms that are sure to come.

WARNING!

Never eat any plant without first knowing important factors:
- Are you certain this is the edible plant you think it is?
- Has it been sprayed with any dangerous substance?
- Are some parts of the plant edible and others not?

QUEEN ANNE'S LACE *daucus carota* (DA kus ka ROW ta). Once this lovely lady enters your garden, she will find her way into all areas of it. I don't mind because I just pull up any of the plants I don't want. Last summer a nice area of our front yard was filled with Queen Anne's Lace. This was the source of the subtly sweet scent drifting across the walk toward our front door. The scent is as fragile as the tiny clusters of white flowers shaped like a snowflake. Queen Anne's Lace makes a lovely addition to a bouquet of cut summer flowers. It is also nice all by itself with a few hosta leaves for contrast.

29

ABOUT GARDENING FRIENDS:

Find some! My garden would not be what it is without the many starters given to me by friends and relatives. I name these flowers after the people who gave them to me: Judy's lamium and feverfew and thyme; Char's coneflower and malva and veronica and more; Leanne's iris and Cathy's vari-colored sedum; Joyce's "Autumn Joy" sedum and silver yarrow (which *she* called "Karen's yarrow"); Mary's peony and iris; Tammy's bleeding heart and pear tree; Kay's dahlias; Karen's white iris and blue iris and Carol's forget-me-nots.

Forget me not is true—I forget them not. This is a garden of my friends.

DAISY *chrysanthemum leucanthemum, etc.* (kriss ANN thuh mum lew KAN thuh mum). Daisy plants are all over our yard. Char calls mine "field" daisies and laughs knowingly. They do pop up all over, but if I don't like them here, I transplant them there—or throw them in the compost pile (or drop them off at a friend's).

There are as many flowers named for boys as for girls: Alexander, Adam's Needle, Jack-in-the-Pulpit, Jacob's Ladder, Joe Pye Weed, and Sweet William.

ASTILBE (ah STILL bee). A regal plant with many varieties. You can have continuous spring to fall bloom with several color choices. I cut down many of the dried plants at the end of our growing season, but leave a few of the astilbe flower plumes for winter interest. A stately sight, astible plumes marching across our winter snows.

CREEPING PHLOX *phlox subulata* (flox sub you LAH tuh) is among the earliest phlox to bloom. It does seem to creep, gradually spreading nicely to blanket whatever area you wish to cover. Mixing colors gives you a multi-colored quilt.

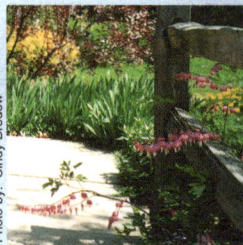

Photo by: Cindy Bredow

BLEEDING HEART *dicentra spectabilis* (dye SEN truh speck TAH bih lis). The dicentra pictured blooms in spring. I also have *dicentra "luxuriant"* in the garden which is everblooming and tends to pop up voluntarily in surprising places.

POPPY *papaver* (pa PAH ver). The opium poppy is the only poppy in our yard. You will not see this variety for sale, but if a friend gives you seeds your garden will never again lack for this beauty. The tiny seeds scatter from the seed pods to bloom the next year. I like to carry seed pods to other areas of the yard, spreading seed in late fall. We are apt to see poppies "pop up" almost anywhere each June.